THE PET DAY MYSTERY

WRITTEN BY MARY BLOUNT CHRISTIAN
ILLUSTRATED BY JOE BODDY

Milliken Publishing Company, St. Louis, Missouri

Cover Design by Henning Design, St. Louis, Missouri

Library of Congress Catalog Card Number: 88-60631
ISBN 0-88335-599-X (pbk.)/ISBN 0-88335-595-7 (lib. bdg.)

Boom! Boom! Thunder shook the windows.
The rain came down fast.
Ann and Walter put on their
yellow raincoats and rain boots.

Ann put her cat Fuzz Face into a cage.
"Come on," she told Walter.
"The bus is here."
She ran out with the cage.

Walter called his dog.
"Come on, Watson!" he said.
"It's Pet Day at school.
This is the best show-and-tell
day of the year."

j 40793

1

"Woof! Woof!" Watson said.
He and Walter ran to the bus.
Ann and Walter climbed on with their pets.

The bus was full of children and pets.
Pedro had his parrot, Noisy.
"Arrrk! Arrrk!" Noisy said.

David had his dog, Barker.
"Woof! Woof!" Barker said.

"Woof! Woof!" Watson said.

"Pfffft!" Fuzz Face said.

"I'm glad Pet Day is only one day a year," the driver said.

At school Ann saw her friend Tina.
Tina had brought two hamsters.
Their names were Wiggles and Tulip.
"They are so little and cute," Ann said.

"But they do not like your cat," Tina said.

Almost everyone brought a pet.
Some pets were in bowls.
Some were in cages.
Others sat by the children.

Dogs barked and cats hissed.
Turtles hid in their shells.
Rabbits hopped in their cages.

"I'm glad Pet Day is only one
day a year," Mrs. Brown said.
"Tell us about your parrot," she told Pedro.

"Noisy came from South America," Pedro said.
"He can say hello and good-bye.
He can fly, and he can
eat raisins from my hand."

"Arrrk! Arrrk!" Noisy said.

"And now we know how he got
his name," Ann said.
The children laughed.

It was Walter's turn.
"Watson is very smart.
He can do tricks.
Sit, Watson," Walter said.
Watson rolled on his back
and kicked his legs.

Walter sat on the floor.
"No, like this," he said.

Ann giggled.
"See how smart Watson is?" she said.
"He has taught Walter to sit."
Everyone laughed.
Walter blushed and sat down.

Ann told the children about her cat.
"Fuzz Face is four years old.
He takes vitamins and goes to
the doctor just like we do.
He likes to eat meat and chase rodents."

Tina wrapped her arms around her cage.
"You mean like hamsters!"
Ann put Fuzz Face in his cage and sat down.

"Don't worry," Walter told Tina.
"Her cat is lazy. He only eats food from a can."

Mrs. Brown said, "It's lunchtime.
See that your animals have food and water.
Then line up to wash your hands
before we go to the lunchroom."

The children fed and watered their pets.
Then they washed their hands
and got their lunch money.
"What about our pets?" Ann asked.
"Will they be all right?"

"Don't worry," Mrs. Brown said.
"I'll close the door."

"Watson will watch them," Walter said.

"That silly dog?" Ann said, laughing.
The class went to the lunchroom.

When they came back from lunch,
Mrs. Brown unlocked the door.
The class went in.

"Let's finish showing our pets," Mrs. Brown said.
"Tina, let's start with you."

Tina gasped. "Oh, no!
The cage door is open!
My hamsters are gone!"
Tina glared at Ann and cried,
"Your cat ate Wiggles and Tulip!"

Ann glared back.
"My cat is in his cage.
Maybe you left the door open
and your hamsters ran away."

Tina started to cry.
"I know I closed the door to the cage."

Pedro stood up. "Uh oh.
Look at Noisy's cage.
I forgot to tell you one
important thing about Noisy...
He can open cage doors."

"I'll never see my hamsters again!" Tina cried.

Ann put her arm around Tina.
"Don't cry, Tina. We will find them."

"Yeah," David said.
"They will be fine."

"But maybe they ran away!" Tina said.
"Maybe they left the room!
They could be far away by now."

Mrs. Brown closed the door.
"They must still be in this room,"
Ann told Tina. "The door was
closed while we were at lunch."

Walter pulled out his notebook and pencil.
"Tell us about your hamsters," he said.
"Pedro, Ann, David, and I will take the case.
We are the Sherlock Street Detectives."

"Well, my hamsters sleep in the day," Tina said.
"They play and eat at night.
They like to snuggle in small places,
and they eat these food pellets."

Walter wrote in his book:

Sleep in day.
up at night.
Snuggle in
small places.
Eat special
pellets

"Let's put down some pellets,"
Pedro said.
"Then we will close the shades and
turn out the lights. It will be dark.
Maybe the hamsters will think
it's night."

21

Tina put food pellets on the floor.
The children pulled down the shades.
Mrs. Brown turned off the light.
"Be very still, children," she said.

They waited and waited.
Then they turned on the lights.
The hamsters were not there.
Tina started to cry again.

"You said the hamsters like to snuggle in small places," Walter said.
"We should look in small places."

j40793

The children looked inside their desks.
There were papers and books,
but there were no hamsters.

24

They looked in the supply boxes.
They found scissors and crayons,
but they did not find hamsters.

They looked in the chalk box.
They found chalk,
but they did not find hamsters.

"We have looked in all the small places,"
Tina said. "My hamsters are gone."

"Look!" David said.
"The door to the coatroom is open.
It's just a crack, but hamsters are small."

The children looked in the
pockets of their raincoats.
Then they looked in their rain boots.
There, snuggled up inside a rain boot,
were Wiggles and Tulip.

Tina put them back in their cage.
"If they are ever lost again," she said,
"I will call the Sherlock Street Detectives."

Glossary

hamsters – Small animals that look like mice, have bags in their cheeks, and have short tails.

parrot – A kind of bird that has a curved bill and a long tail. Most parrots have bright feathers. Some parrots copy the sounds that they hear.

pellets – Little, hard pieces of something. Pellets are shaped like a ball or a bullet.

rodents – Animals with large front teeth used to bite at something again and again to wear it away. Rats and mice are rodents.

snuggle – To curl up in a warm, safe place.

vitamins – Things that keep animals and plants healthy.

Vocabulary

almost	closed	gasped	notebook	shells	tricks
animals	coatroom	giggled	others	Sherlock	Tulip
Ann	crack	glared	papers	shook	turned
arm(s)	crayons	gone	parrot	silly	turtles
around	cried	hamsters	Pedro	smart	unlocked
barked	dark	hissed	pellets	snuggle	vitamins
Barker	David	important	pencil	snuggled	Walter
blushed	desks	kicked	places	South America	watch
bowls	detectives	laughed	pockets	special	water
brought	doctor	laughing	pulled	started	watered
cage(s)	door(s)	lazy	rabbits	stood	Watson
case	driver	left	raincoats	street	while
chalk	everyone	lunch	raisins	supply	Wiggles
chase	finish	lunchroom	rodents	taught	windows
children	floor	lunchtime	rolled	think	worry
class	found	money	scissors	thunder	wrapped
climbed	friend	Mrs. Brown	shades	Tina	year(s)
close	Fuzz Face	noisy			